NATURE DETECTIVES

A Walk by the River

Jo Waters

Raintree

Chicago, Illinois

D1318458

© 2006 Raintree
a division of Reed Elsevier Inc.
Chicago, Illinois

Customer Service   888–454–2279

Visit our website at www.heinemannlibrary.com

All rights reserved. No part of this publication may be reproduced or transmitted in
any form or by any means, electronic or mechanical, including photocopying, recording, taping, or
any information storage and retrieval system, without permission in writing from the publisher.

Photo research by Maria Joannou and Rebecca Sodergren
Designed by Jo Hinton-Malivoire and Tinstar Design Ltd (www.tinstar.co.uk)
Printed and bound in China by South China Printing Company
10 09 08 07 06
10 9 8 7 6 5 4 3 2 1

Library of Congress Cataloging-in-Publication Data
Waters, Jo.
  A walk by the river / Jo Waters.
    p. cm. -- (Nature detectives)
  Includes index.
  ISBN 1-4109-2292-8 (library binding-hardcover) -- ISBN 1-4109-2297-9 (pbk.)
  1. Rivers--Juvenile literature. I. Title.
  QH97.W38 2006
  578.76'4--dc22
                                    2005029319

Acknowledgments
The Publishers would like to thank the following for permission to reproduce photographs:
Alamy Images/Brian Shadwell; Alamy Images/Colin Pickett p. 17; Alamy Images/David Boag p. 11;
Alamy Images/Doug Wilson p. 15; Alamy Images/M Timothy O'Keefe p. 16; Alamy/PhotoStockFile p.
14; Corbis p. 23; Digital Vision p. 12; p. 5; FLPA/Cisca Castelijns/Foto Natura p. 9; FLPA/Gerry
Ellis/Minden Pictures; FLPA/Michael Quinton/Minden Pictures p. 21; Harcourt Education Ltd/Malcolm
Harris pp. 4, 7; NHPA/Andy Rouse p. 19; NHPA/Ernie Janes p. 18; NHPA/Robert Thompson p. 8;
Photolibrary/ Oxford Scientific Films p. 6, 10, 13, 22.

Cover photograph reproduced with permission of Corbis/Ron Watts.

Our thanks to Annie Davy and Michael Scott for their assistance in the preparation of this book.

Every effort has been made to contact copyright holders of any material reproduced in this book.
Any omissions will be rectified in subsequent printings if notice is given to the publisher.

Some words are shown in bold, **like this**. You can find out
what they mean by looking in the glossary.

Contents

Along the Riverbank

Where are we?
We are by the river!

4

The water **ripples** and the sunlight **sparkles**.

5

Reeds and Cattails

Reeds **sway** in the **breeze**.

6

Cattails have thick, velvety heads.

Dragonflies

Dragonflies are a type of **insect**.

Its wings are see-through.

Trees and Flowers

Trees bend over the water.

Colorful flowers grow.

Frogs

A frog sits in the water.

Those legs are great
for jumping.
Hop hop!

Under the Water

Minnows look like little arrows in the water.

Bigger fish swim in the river, too.

Fishing for Food

This heron is fishing.

Dinnertime! He just caught a fish.

17

Riverbank Families

Goslings look like little balls of fluff.

They are great swimmers.

Playtime

Otters swim in
the water.

They play together.

Good-bye River

A deer comes to drink
the water.

Take one last look.
Time to go home.

Glossary

breeze light wind
gosling baby goose
insect small animal with six legs

ripples has small waves
sparkles reflects the light
sway move slowly from side to side

Index

Notes for adults

Exploring the natural world at an early age can help promote awareness of the environment and general understanding of life processes. Discussing the seasons with children can be a good way of helping them understand the concepts of time, patterns, and change. Identifying features that people share with insects and animals can promote understanding of similarities.

Follow-up activities
• Encourage children to think and talk about why people should take care of the environment and not damage plants or harm animals.
• Ask children to describe the sounds they might hear by a river.
• Use the animals featured in the book to get children moving. Ask them to show you how fish, frogs, and dragonflies move.